HarperCollins®, 🐾®, and I Can Read Book® are
trademarks of HarperCollins Publishers Inc.

Dumpy to the Rescue!
Text and illustrations copyright © 2004 by Dumpy, LLC
Printed in the U.S.A. All rights reserved.
www.harperchildrens.com

Library of Congress Cataloging-in-Publication Data
Edwards, Julie Andrews, date.
Dumpy to the rescue! / by Julie Andrews Edwards and Emma Walton Hamilton ;
illustrated by Tony Walton with Cassandra Boyd
    p. cm. — (My first I can read book)
    Summary: After bringing dinner to some of his farm animal friends, Dumpy helps
Mama Goat search the farm for her missing baby.
    ISBN 0-06-052689-0 — ISBN 0-06-052690-4 (lib. bdg.) — ISBN 0-06-052691-2 (pbk.)
    [1. Dump trucks—Fiction. 2. Trucks—Fiction. 3. Goats—Fiction. 4. Missing
Children—Fiction. 5. Domestic Animals—Fiction. 6. Farm life—Fiction.]
I. Hamilton, Emma Walton. II. Walton, Tony, ill. III. Boyd, Cassandra, ill.
IV. Title. V. Series.
PZ7.E2562 Dv 2004   2002152613
[E]—dc21   CIP
                                                                          AC

1 2 3 4 5 6 7 8 9 10
❖
First Edition

Dumpy to the Rescue!

By Julie Andrews Edwards and Emma Walton Hamilton
Illustrated by Tony Walton
with Cassandra Boyd

HarperCollins*Publishers*

Broom! Broom!

Dinnertime!

Dumpy has hay for the cows.

Broom! Broom!

Dumpy has oats for the horse.

Look out, chicks!

Here is your corn.

Hello, goats!

Here is your corn and hay.

But where is Baby Goat?

He will miss his dinner.

Toot! Toot!

Dumpy will find Baby Goat.
Mama and Papa Goat
will go too.

Is he in the shed?

Baa! Mama Goat calls.

No. No baby in the shed.

But who ate all the nuts?

Is he by the pond?

No. But here is dinner
for the ducks.

Uh-oh!

Who ate all the baby roses?

Is Baby Goat at the house?

No. But where is the cat's milk?

Brooom! Brooom!

Is Baby Goat with the pigs?

No.

But here is your dinner, pigs!

Oh, no! Who ate Pop-Up's hat?

Where can that Baby Goat be?
He *must* want his dinner!

Toot! Toot!

Where are you, Baby Goat?

Oh, my!

Who ate all the apples?

Let's look in Dumpy's barn!

Here he is! Uh-oh!

Now we know who ate it all.

Baby Goat had *lots* of dinner.

Silly billy!

Sleep well!